Hootlet Home

Hootlet Home

BERTHA CROW

Illustrated by Harry Baerg

REVIEW AND HERALD PUBLISHING ASSOCIATION
WASHINGTON, D.C.

CHAPTER 1

1468843

Papa and mamma owl winged their way silently through the woods. They kept mostly to the brush, along the barbed-wire fence, mingling with the shadows. Beyond this was the narrow opening with only a bush or two, and at the edge, showing sandy white in the night, twisted the crooked road. Any minute now lights would be springing up in the house across the way. The full moon glittered on the peaceful marsh.

As the moon went down there was a pearly gray in the heavens to the east. Soon it would be sunrise, and mamma and papa owl must find sleeping quarters for the day. They quickly flew to a gnarled old sycamore tree not far from the road.

It rained and sleeted and snowed, and the wind whistled around the trees. But the owls were prepared. They simply hugged the sheltered side of the tree.

HOOTLET HOME

With one last gentle *Whoo-whooo-whoooo* for each other, mamma and papa owl lifted their fluffy, feathery, earlike tufts above their heads, snuggled against the trunk, and went to sleep.

And in the big, comfortable house across the way, Pansy heard their last hooting call, shivered for a moment, pulled the covers closer over her ears, and went back to sleep. Nor in her dreams was there the slightest hint of warning that the future held owlish adventures.

Through the day a sharp, blustery storm set in, with all the force and fury of midwinter. It rained and sleeted and snowed, and the wind whistled around the trees. Poor papa and mamma owl! But the Creator has prepared the owls for surprises such as these. They simply stepped around to the south side of the trunk. Here they were sheltered from the wind. They fluffed out their soft, feathery coats and kept fairly warm. And even though the snow swirled and drifted and practically covered them, thick layers of fat kept the cold away.

HOOTLET HOME

Dark came early, for the clouds were low. The moon and the stars were hidden from view. But once more the owls were astir. They opened their black-and-yellow eyes, sang their *Whoo-whooo-whoooo, whoo-whooo-whoooo* softly, and flew to the barn behind the house. The downy edge along their wing feathers helped them to go quietly, and unsuspecting mice were startled in their scurrying trip to the corn bin. With beaks snapping, the owls carried their victims to the top of the hollow tree, there to enjoy their meal.

Whoo-whooo, whoo-whooo, sounded their deep, hollow hooting, seeming to come from several different places at once, and Pansy again stirred in her sleep as the owls went about the business of setting up a home.

Papa and mamma owl finally found an old nest high in an oak tree. It was a huge tree with many knots and tiny twigs, but that made it all the better. The nest was little more than a clump of old sticks and dried grass. But since they would not build one of their own, they set about

8

making this one as warm and soft as possible.

Mamma owl plucked a feather from her breast. She put it in a worn, thin place. She plucked another and another. She padded here. She padded there. She sat in the nest, trying it out, turning around and around.

Papa owl watched while she did all the work. But he did sit protectingly near on a limb close by. Then, as if displeased with his idleness, mamma owl flew up, gave a smart tweak with her beak, and pulled several of his breast feathers. With a surprised *whoo-whooo*, he watched as mamma owl settled down on the nest. But later, when there were three white oval eggs in the nest, he forgave her completely.

Papa owl looked over their new location. Their sturdy oak tree was standing right beside the twisting, sandy road. In fact, some of its spreading branches practically reached across. A little later that would be no problem, but right now, with the branches still bare, they might be seen by man. Still, the nest had been there

H. BAERG

Papa owl hooted worriedly as he surveyed the surroundings. The bare
branches provided little or no covering for the nest.

for years, and people were used to it. But a new family lived in the big house now, and papa owl hooted worriedly. There were two houses nearby —the big white one to the south, and a smaller one to the north, at the bend of the road, facing the knotted oak tree. Houses meant barns nearby. And barns meant mice and rats and chickens for easy food.

Then, there was the marsh. The great oak's branches spread over part of it, too, on the west. There would be many little creatures coming to drink. And farther west was the thicket where papa and mamma owl had weathered the storm in the sycamore tree. Toward the south the marsh crossed the road and wormed its way through the cornfields, the meadows, the cotton fields, and the peas. Papa owl could see thick underbrush growing in the marsh as it wound its way behind the big house, full of sassafras bushes, persimmon sprouts, alders, and blackberry vines that would offer excellent protection when they were thick with leaves. This meant rabbits and squirrels, too. No, they were not likely to go hungry.

And right there, practically on the farmer's lawn, was the old dead tree where he and mamma owl had eaten their meal last night. But he must not worry any more, for pale tinted streaks of red in the east showed that morning was not far away.

CHAPTER 2

In a cozy bedroom in the big white house Pansy awakened early. She saw the crimson colors turn to gold and watched the sun make of dewdrops a thousand glittering sparkles on spears of grass. Mother hens were scratching worms, with inviting clucks to their chicks. Father whistled in the barn, stripped the shucks from nubbin ears of corn, and fed the mares. Mother was already at the family wash, soapsuds up to her elbows in frothy whiteness.

But Pansy was not busy. She sat listlessly on the edge of the bed and dangled her socks to the floor. She had a drowsy, sleepy feeling and wished she could go back to sleep. Over the way, past the crook in the road, she could hear a cow-

2

bell tinkling. That would be Margaret driving the cows home.

Margaret lived in the little house with Mother Hinds. Sometimes cows could be stubborn and forget to come at milking time, even in spite of their bawling babies. So Margaret would usually bring Blackie, and Pansy would drive Bess, giving them a smart whack across the back to hurry them along.

Then suddenly sleep vanished and Pansy was in a hurry. Shoes and socks were on in a jiffy.

"I must have heard owls all night, to make me sleep this late in the morning," she grumbled. "Wish they'd take their hooting someplace else besides right in my ear. Now Margaret's ahead of me, and I'll have to go get Bess by myself."

She could not resist a run through the hall and down the back porch. Her steps sounded bumpety, bump, bump, in the crisp, cold air. But Bess was already milked and turned out to pasture. That meant that the tinkling she had heard was Margaret's cow going back to pasture. The

14

baby calves stood at the fence, looking longingly at their mothers' retreating forms and emitting baby bellows and licking their muzzles.

Pansy hated to lose a moment of the new day, but her room had to be cleaned. Not even a wrinkle must be seen in the spread, and mother held her firmly to the task. Only then could she enjoy the pleasures of the day.

She flew to the kitchen for breakfast. Mother had it warming on the oven. My, but she was hungry!

"Slow down, Pansy," cautioned mother as she watched her daughter gulp down her food. "You're going to choke yourself, and you can't play at all then."

Pansy tried, but in a few moments she was down the steps. Suddenly she stopped short; she almost sat down.

"Shoo, shoo! You bad old hens," she shouted, and recovering from her shock, ran pell-mell into the yard. Feathers flew everywhere amid squawks and croaks of indignation. With quivering lips,

15

With quivering lips, Pansy rescued Ohio, her dolly, from under the silver-maple tree. And what a sight she was, her face all blistered and peeling!

HOOTLET HOME

Pansy rescued Ohio, her dolly, from under the silver maple tree. And what a sight she was! Her face was all blistered and peeling where each dew-drop had rested the night before. Not that she played with Ohio any more, but she didn't want the chickens pecking her eyes out either!

Mother, hearing the commotion, left her wash and hurried around the corner. She took in the situation at a glance. "You'll have to learn to put your toys away," she said gently. She noticed two little tears that insisted on rolling down Pansy's cheeks no matter how hard she tried to squeeze them back. Soon the tears were overflowing fast, but Pansy felt better because of them. Leaving the dolly with mother, she ran out the gate.

The grass on the lawn was young and green. A plank bridge crossed the ditch, and as she tripped lightly over she noticed that the water was almost gone. She wished it would have stayed longer. Mother wouldn't let her go barefooted yet, and she did like to wade in the water and to feel the mud squishing and oozing up between her toes. Why, oh, why, wouldn't mother let her go wading?

Pansy had already forgotten that it had been snowing yesterday, for the snow was gone now. The trees had a feathery, springlike look. The day was fresh and fragrant, and the birds were out for an airing, glad that cold, hungry days were soon to be gone, glad to be flying about and building again.

Pansy listened to the sandy crunch as she skipped along. After she had gone a short distance down the road she turned to look at her home. It always made her feel comfortable to view it from a distance, peaceful and sunny, solid and secure, something to rest upon. Though the paint was peeling a little, the house was still attractive as it spread over a slight knoll. She could see the rambler rosebush at the corner of the front porch and the blooming jonquils. The garden seemed to give off a spicy fragrance. Pansy loved her home.

But here was Margaret, turning her great

eyes and rolling them from side to side. Each of her kinky pigtails stood separately, dancing up and down with her skinny arms and legs.

"Don't you know what day this is?" she asked as they met under papa and mamma owl's old oak tree.

"Monday, of course," answered Pansy, aware that something was different, but what she didn't know.

"Course it's Monday," said Margaret. "But what else?"

"The—let me see," Pansy put her finger to her cheek in mock thoughtfulness. "Yesterday was the fourteenth. It must be——" Her eyes brightened as light dawned. She sat flat down in the dust, right in the middle of the road.

"It's the fifteenth! Mother's birthday!" she cried.

"And your mother always lets us go barefooted on her birthday," affirmed Margaret, wiggling her little black toes in the cool shady dust.

"Ouch! Ouch! Oh, my foot!" she suddenly screamed, dancing around
on one foot and holding the other with her hand.

HOOTLET HOME

"Let's play tag," suggested Pansy as she stuffed her socks in the toe of her shoes and set them on a root. She wiggled her toes in the dust for a moment, feeling its soft smoothness. "I'll be first," and so saying, she darted after Margaret, who quickly touched wood. Touching wood, they were safe, but Margaret left safety and dashed for a dead limb in the ditch.

"Ouch! Ouch! Oh, my foot!" she suddenly screamed, dancing around on one foot and holding the other with her hands. A sharp, jagged thorn had pierced the tender flesh and buried itself so deeply that they could not pull it out.

Papa owl awoke with a start even though it was broad daylight. "Huh, huh," he said questioningly. Luckily for him, between Margaret's cries of pain and Pansy's comforting words he was not heard.

Mother Hinds poked her head out the door. "What have you done now, Margaret?" she asked, hurrying down the road as fast as she could go. "What ails you, child? I told you it's too soon to go barefooted," she scolded tenderly. "I don't care if it *is* Mrs. Griffin's birthday!" So saying, she sat down on the ditch bank, took the little foot in her hands, and carefully looked at the end of the ugly black thorn.

"Grit your teeth, Margaret. This is going to hurt," she said, and taking a needle from her apron front, proceeded to pick.

Margaret cried, Mother Hinds soothed. Pansy sympathized, and papa owl in his tree wondered which was worse—the chattering of the squirrels, the screams of the blue jays, the scolding of the robins, or the cries, antics, and laughter of earth-bound people. These woodsy folk would have pestered him, but at least, he would not have feared them.

Mother Hinds, with one last dig, pried out the thorn and dabbed at the blood that oozed out.

"No more play for you today, honey child," she said, and gathering her sobbing little girl in her big arms, carefully carried her home.

22

CHAPTER 3

It was warmer now, and the tender buds had grown to leaves. They offered a covering for the home in the treetop, and fear eased in papa owl's heart. The owls hooted freely at night and slept securely in the day.

The baby owlets were hatched. Mamma and papa owl had kept them warm, each taking a turn on the eggs, until three almost-bare, white-downed babies clamored for food. Their eyes were shut at first, but by the time they were about a week old they could stare with all the serious-ness of their parents. Soon yellowish rings ap-peared around the black centers of their eyes. At the end of three weeks their feathers began to show colors of buff, gray, and dull brown, with a

The baby owlets were hatched. Mamma and papa owl had kept them warm, each taking a turn on the eggs, until three babies clamored for food.

white patch at the throat. Their tufts began to develop, with a blackish-brown edging the tips.

Such appetites babies have! And the little hootlets were no exception. Mamma and papa owl went abroad in the warm nights, alive with the sounds of nature. They could not see the beetles and moths and other creatures but their sharp, slanted ears, hidden under the tufts, directed them to the food. The babies could not swallow mice, rats, and larger creatures, so the parents sat on the branches and with their short, hooked beaks tore their catch into bite-sized bits.

As the days grew longer, companies of blackbirds swarmed the marshy places, swaying on the reeds and calling messages to one another with shrilling voices. Some sported brilliant red patches on their sleek, black wings. Pansy and Margaret ran among them, swinging and flailing their arms, and screaming just as shrilly as the birds, merely to hear the commotion. But more often the girls wandered to the great oak tree, there to build their castles in the sand. Yards, too, they built. They made doors in their castle walls and furnished each room.

But high in the nest things were not so serene. The little owlets were growing and pushing.

Chee-ee, chee-ee, they quarreled. *Squee-aw,* they squalled. The mixture of squalls and screeches resounded through the nights. Like naughty children, each vied for the larger share of food. Selfish and moody, they were, and the nest was simply too full of owls. Someone had to go. But the big, handsome one with the pretty black and buff, snapped his hooked beak angrily, fluffed his feathers importantly, and determined that it should not be he. His timid little sister or drab, silent brother had better be careful or they would find themselves without a home. The brave bold one raised his tufts, not yet fully developed. He strutted around and around the nest, pushing rudely as he went. His attitude invited trouble, and it came to the little hootlet just as surely as it comes to boys and girls who bully their way in the world. His selfishness was about

26

to be rewarded. He hopped dangerously near the edge, daring anyone to cross him. Tempted to overestimate his strength, and puffed up with pride, he hopped to a dangerous spot on the edge of the nest. Suddenly the soft summer wind puffed against the fluff of feathers. He went toppling over the side, fluttering and fighting for balance on one of the limbs so swiftly passing by. But his claws could not sufficiently bite into the bark, and he came to a screeching halt on his handsome white chest.

Dazed and shaken from his fall, wings and feathers torn, he crept over a fallen branch, followed its shadow to a prickly thornbush, and hid away.

Papa and mamma owl frantically flapped and scolded and grieved. But they could not change the situation. And even as a mother never forsakes her children, so papa and mamma owl still cared for their child. Even though the job was harder and more risky, they brought tidbits and, if possible, better morsels for their wayward

Suddenly the soft summer wind puffed against the fluff of feathers. He went toppling over the side, fluttering and fighting for a hold on a passing limb.

son. They flitted across the moonlight and fluttered around him, singing *Whoo-whooo-whoooo* softly. But when the sun rose, they flew to the lowest limbs, closed their great eyes, and went to sleep.

Poor little one. All he could do was nurse his bruises and try to sleep too. But it was impossible in a strange place, and as the sun rose, hot and blinding, strange noises disturbed him. He dared not make a move, for his safe nest was far away. He missed his sister and brother, even the quarreling! If he could only get home again! Suddenly, before him were strange-looking objects; two pairs of legs—one pair black and the other white.

"This must be Africa," Margaret was saying. "Watch out for tigers and lions. We'll catch the monkeys, though. We'll sell them for pets."

But Pansy was far down the trail. "Let's follow this. Maybe it leads to the mission."

"But we're safe here," insisted Margaret, rolling her eyes. "If we go any farther we might run into cannibals you're always talking about."

3

His safe nest was far away. Suddenly, before him were strange-looking objects; two pairs of legs—one black and the other white.

"Well, that's what we're here for, sister. Don't you know we're going to make Christians of them? Besides, we have no food," reasoned Pansy sensibly. "And no water either. We'll die for sure, here. We'd better move on. Watch for snakes now."

Margaret pretended to shudder in terror as she followed her companion. At the edge of the marsh they hesitated. "Let's turn back," pleaded Margaret, her twisted pigtails bobbing with each step. "There are likely to be alligators in the swamps. I know there are." Shafts of sunlight trailed across the marsh, making silver glitter on the water.

"Sh-sh," cautioned Pansy. "Be quiet. You'll scare the animals."

"What animals?" questioned Margaret indignantly. This make-believe play was beginning to seem quite senseless to her. "I don't see any animals. And you don't either."

"Well, you just wait," answered Pansy, flopping down on her stomach, her feet stretched out behind, toes practically touching the little owlet as he crouched farther under the bush. He was so stiff with fright he dared not move.

Margaret grumbled and flopped down too, peering intently into the bush.

"There's a wild boar," whispered Pansy as a white pig with pink skin and a very curly tail waddled down to drink.

"Humph," grumbled Margaret. "Been seeing them all my life."

"Use your imagination," commanded Pansy. "We're missionaries in Africa. You said so your-self. Remember?" Pansy wiggled in excitement, sending her toes farther under the bush. They were touching the owl's breast feathers now, but she didn't notice.

"There's a hippopotamus," observed Marga-ret obligingly as an old mulley cow waded up to her ankles and took long, cool draughts. The girls giggled as they watched her tail flip the flies off.

"No, that's a rhinoceros," contradicted Pansy with authority. "Ye-ee-ow," she ended as she realized her toes were wiggling up and down in a soft, feathery something.

At the same instant the hootlet in timidity and fear thrashed around, trying to escape, but he was tightly pinned.

Whoo-whooo-whoooo, he cried softly.

Margaret looked at Pansy thoughtfully.

"What's that?" questioned Pansy, her eyes as big and as round as ever Margaret's were.

"What's what? I didn't hear anything. Your imagination! Who's scaring away all the animals now?" Margaret looked unconcernedly across the shimmering blue water.

But Pansy was on her feet. "Something's under that bush, I tell you. And I'm going to see what it is."

At first she could see nothing, so well did the little fellow mingle with the shadows, but as her eyes became accustomed to the dimness, Pansy spied the handsome black-and-buff owlet.

"What is it, Margaret? Come and see!" she called excitedly, trying to get a better view.

33

Margaret took a turn and peered closer. The little owlet stared right back.

"I don't know," she answered. "But I'll go get mother. She'll know what it is. You wait here! Don't let it get away." And Margaret sped away.

Her mother came puffing back. "What have you found now, honey child? It beats all how you're always poking around in bushes." Then she caught sight of the frightened little creature. "Why, it's one of the owls I been hearing. A baby one, sure is!"

"Get him out, Auntie. I want him," said Pansy, trying to get at him herself. But Mother Hinds jerked her back.

"He'll take your fingers off, child. Wait. Let me see." Mother Hinds took off her white apron and tossed it carefully over the small round head. Though he thrashed and scratched and screeched, he could not get out. Pansy picked him up and took him home.

"Get him out, Auntie. I want him," said Pansy, trying to get at him
herself. But Mother Hinds jerked her back.

CHAPTER 4

At first mother protested. But Pansy pleaded, and mother gave in.

"But whatever will we do with an owl in the house?" she asked of no one in particular. She looked worriedly around her home, trying to imagine muddy tracks on her clean spreads.

But at the moment Pansy was thoughtfully considering the fate of the little bundle of feathers held lovingly in the folds of Auntie's apron.

"I declare," mother was continuing, "I can't see why you aren't satisfied with a respectable cat, or some other animal that was intended for a pet. No, you have to have weird creatures like an owl. What was it you had last time? Rats?"

"But they were white ones, Mother," answered Pansy. "And intended for pets," she reminded. Her eyes clouded for a moment as she remembered how their cat had eaten them after it clawed the latch open.

Mother watched the look on Pansy's face. She had meant to be kind, but there had been scolding in her words. Suddenly she laughed. "Never mind, honey, you take in all the little things your heart desires. We'll find room for them somewhere."

So the frightened little owl was turned loose in the pea pantry, where a timid little brown bunny already lived. Pansy had a natural love for things of the wild and a more-than-natural way with them. They always thrived under her care and seemed not too unhappy.

"What are you going to name him?" asked mother as they stood in the doorway. Pansy watched with dreamy eyes as the young owl tried his feet again and flopped around with his torn wings.

"Herman," answered Pansy.

37

"I sure hope you don't keep him long," said Margaret, holding a long,
red, wiggling worm between her thumb and forefinger.

HOOTLET HOME

"You know you'll have to feed him," mother reminded. "You'd better get started collecting so he can eat tonight."

"What will I collect?" asked Pansy.

"Oh, anything," answered mother. "Worms and bugs, most likely." Herman, who had backed into the darkest corner, closed his dark, yellow-rimmed eyes and went to sleep.

"Oh, perhaps the light hurts his eyes," said Pansy, at last slipping away to get Margaret's help in digging worms and catching anything they could for Herman's supper. Or perhaps he might consider it breakfast. Whichever it was, he had to eat.

"I sure hope you don't keep him long," said Margaret, holding a long, red, wiggling worm between her thumb and forefinger.

"Who?" asked Pansy.

"Herman, that's who," said Margaret, the worm still dangling between her thumb and finger.

"Why?" asked Pansy.

"Because I don't like to hold these slimy things, that's why."

Pansy laughed and sat on the back steps to catch her breath. She mopped her forehead. "Maybe I should let him go. But not until he's well again." And once more she took up the hunt.

Margaret tired of the food-gathering and set off through the back gate and down the trail toward home.

"You must fix him a cage," reminded mother as the sun began to set. "It's almost time for him to wake up. Little Brown Bunny will wake up too, and we can't have them both running around together. That would surely mean tragedy."

Instantly Pansy was alert. She hadn't thought of that. But she had no idea how to go about building an owl house. "If only Buba or Harold were older," she sighed, "they'd build one for me."

It was a great trial in Pansy's young life that she could never build a thing, and she was distressed more than once because the many doll beds, rocking chairs, and other dreamy adventures in carpentry, wobbled, toppled, and fell over when she had barely finished with them. Try as she might, she could not fashion a cage. So when Herman awoke, fluttered around, and emitted his soft *Whoo-whoooo-whooo*, Pansy took him to her room, shut the doors, and turned him loose.

The trouble was, she shared the room with Lois and Te, and they were sure to object to having their bedposts used as a roost.

"We don't run a zoo, you know," Te remarked, looking at Herman as she put on her nightie.

"And I don't like the way he looks at me," Do shivered. (She was trying to be dignified and wanted everyone to call her Lois, but no one ever did.) She jumped into bed and covered up her head.

"You're going to have to clean up in the morning, I'm not," said Te, and with that she too got into bed, yawning sleepily.

"Well," sighed Pansy, "that wasn't as bad as

I expected." Smiling to herself, she turned down the light.

But poor Herman followed the walls, flew into the windows, disregarded his injured wing. In vain he searched for a way of escape. His keen ears caught all the night sounds. He saw the moon rise over the barn, making mysterious shadows. Stars twinkled and pierced the darkness. Herman saw the mists rise over the marsh and heard his brother and sister *chee-eeing* and *squee-awing* and his parents answering softly. But he was in prison, and there was no escape.

If she had known, Pansy's heart would have gone out to him. She would have understood his nervous walking. She would have set him free. But, of course, she did not see, for she was fast asleep. At last Herman perched atop the high old organ, gave one last stare at the owl in the mirror, closed his sad, yellow eyes, and fell asleep, his night of watching behind. That's where he was when Pansy awoke. And Pansy wondered whether he had moved at all.

42

HOOTLET HOME

As soon as prayers were said, breakfast over, and she could decently do so, Pansy took the wicker basket the kittens had outgrown, filled it with soft fluffy strings and rags from mother's quilt box, and put Herman in his new nest. She did not close the top, so he was free to come and go as he chose. For a time this was perfect, for hardly anyone knew he was on the place. He slept all day, only opening his eyes for a halfway peek when anyone came too near. But as he grew stronger and his wing mended, something else had to be done. "Just a little longer, Herman, and you can go free," said Pansy affectionately, busily working with a string in her hand.

It was early morning, with dew still on the ground. Birds twittered, and the world was still a pearly gray in the predawn light. Smoke rose a darker gray over the countryside, for farm folk are early risers and breakfast is over by sunup.

"What are you doing?" asked mother, curiously looking out the door. She had heard voices and came out to investigate. She thought no one

At last Herman perched atop the high old organ, gave one last stare at the owl in the mirror, and closed his sad, yellow eyes and fell asleep.

was awake but herself, and she was surprised to see Pansy and Herman.

"I'm letting Herman get some exercise, Mother," answered Pansy as she deftly slipped a loop over his left foot and tossed him high into the air. Pansy let out string as he flew.

The harvest came and went. Pansy and Herman, who was now her almost constant companion, except when he had to have some sleep, kept the trail busy as they went back and forth between house and field. She carried water and extra tidbits for the men, and Herman rode cluckingly on her shoulders. He eyed with longing the old, craggy trees that grew in the marsh, the dried pods, and vivid leaves. Birds flying and geese honking were almost unbearable, but not once did he try to fly away, for by this time he well knew that he could go only so far with that string fastened around his foot.

Soon the snowy-white cotton bolls had all been picked. The bales and bales had been turned into currency for the winter needs. Stalks had been

4

plowed under for winter decay. The birds gathered to talk over their yearly migration, and the grasshopper's melody and the katydid's music was stilled. The brown, dry cornstalks rustled in the wind, and peas rattled in their brittle pods. The nights became frosty. Gradually the chilly days were interspersed with rain, and gray clouds enveloped the world in a gloomy atmosphere. The cold north wind whistled threateningly with a hint of snow.

Herman should have been content with free food and dry lodging, but wild nature is not easily tamed, and Herman still dreamed of his woodland home. Opportunity always comes to the patient, and a chance to attain this dream came quite unexpectedly. He could hear mother coming. She was checking on the girls. They were sleeping soundly, but they just would close all the windows, and mother believed in having plenty of fresh air even if it was getting wintertime. She raised them halfway, banked the coals in the fireplace, and retired to her own room across the hall.

HOOTLET HOME

Herman supposed it was no use, but he had to try that window. His spirit of sticking to a thing could easily be admired, for he had tried so often before. He supposed this too was a useless attempt, but he must try and try again. Wonder of wonders! The screen was unhooked. The girls had been cleaning in the morning and must have left it open.

Pansy heard it bang as Herman slipped through. But supposing it was the wind showing off, she snuggled under the covers again.

Herman flew silently to the north yard fence. Perched atop the post, curling his claws against it, he tried to get the lay of the land. Yes, there was the tree where mamma and papa owl had first had their supper. He had seen it many times from Pansy's window. And farther north was his home nest in the partially bare oak tree. His family was all gone now with the exception of maybe a brother, who would claim the territory for his own. If Herman even so much as flew across he would probably have to fight.

HOOTLET HOME

The air was getting fresher and sharp, ruffling the white on his throat. Clouds floated across the sky. Herman flew to the thornbush across the road, carefully avoiding the stickers. Here he was able to get a better view of the faraway woods. Even in the occasional moonglow they looked more inviting than before.

But something went wrong. As he hopped off his perch for a long flight, he was jerked to a short halt that plummeted him toward the ground, head over heels, in a flurry of feathers. The string! In his joy he had forgotten it! It had tangled itself around one of the thorns. But worse still, it was just long enough for Herman to be suspended in midair. He flopped, helpless, as he twisted in his efforts to free himself.

But God watches over His little woodsy creatures and He worked in Herman's behalf. The wind, which had been so sharp before, grew to stormlike fury. It bellowed and blew in mighty gusts that laid the grass flat, then paused as though to watch it straighten before puffing again.

HOOTLET HOME

Having spent himself in useless effort, Herman hung limp and forlorn, blown to and fro by the wind. The little thornbush swished and sighed as it whipped from side to side. Herman was bumped against the ground as the wind paused, then swung high in the air again. It seemed useless to fight any more, but with one last great effort he flew with the wind as it slung him upward, and he managed to get his perch on the limb again.

That was much better, but still he was not free. However, it took only a few frantic pecks with his beak to tear the string away. What if his leg was bleeding? It mattered not. He was free! And trembling with eagerness, the wise owl gave one last look at his captive home and flew straight for the black forest that lined the horizon. For the first time in his life he felt like the great horned owl that he was, truly the tiger of the air.

When morning came, there was great excitement at Pansy's house. Such running around and calling, "Herman, Herman." But Herman

But something went wrong. As he hopped off his perch for a long flight, he was jerked to a short halt that plummeted him toward the ground, head over heels.

was far away and could not hear. Nor would he have come if he had heard. He was enjoying his first freedom sleep in many, many months. The great ache in his heart at last was eased.

"Here's his string," Do cried, running around the house. "I found it out in the thornbush."

At sight of it Pansy cried, but mother comforted her. "At least you know he won't be tangled up somewhere starving to death," she said. "And he's perfectly able to take care of himself. Don't grieve for him, dear. Pretty soon you'll have another pet to take his place."

"I know, but it won't be Herman," Pansy sobbed. "Will he ever come back?"

"I doubt it, Pansy," soothed mother. "But if he does, would you honestly want to tie him up again?" Mother looked deep into Pansy's eyes. "Would you?"

The decision was a hard one, since there was just as great an ache in Pansy's heart as had been in Herman's. Pansy dropped her head on mother's breast and cried. "No, I wouldn't catch him," she

51

sobbed. "But, oh, I'll never, never have another Herman! Didn't he know I loved him, Mother?"

"Of course, he did, dear. I'm sure of it. But he loved his woods, too, and the streams and moon and all the night sounds and freedom. We cannot change what God has already planned, and He intended that Herman and all his kind should live in the woods. But we can look forward to heaven, can't we? It will be especially wonderful for you. You can run and play with anything you want to, and the little woods creatures won't ever run away."

And Margaret too offered help in her own little way. "You do beat all, Pansy, how you keep moaning about a little old owl. Don't you know the woods are full of them? Come on, let's play!"

Of course, Margaret felt the loss keenly too, for anything that affected her little white friend, affected her. But she wanted to help, and she figured the best way to do it was to make Pansy busy again so she'd forget about Herman.

Pansy was comforted, but just in case Herman

was near and trying to come home, she wandered around the bend in the road, followed the marsh, peered in the thickets, and like a little lost thing kept calling, calling. And not once during the long, cold winter was the soft mating *Whoo-whooo* heard, or the quarrelsome *chee-ee* of the young, or the shrill screech of capture.

But Herman had been busy. Taking advantage of the few remaining days of perfect weather, he wooed his mate among the showering acorns, the falling nuts, and the turning leaves. He would protect and help and live with her as long as they both lived. He preened his gray feathers, raised his handsome tufts, and screeched as loud as he could. That would teach Cousin Hoot to stay out of his way.

Herman and his mate took possession of an old hollow tree and peered contentedly from the lofty interior through a decayed knothole. Sometimes Herman would perch on a broken snag and survey his domain, daring any to enter. They found food among the spicy pines where the

Herman and his mate took possession of an old hollow tree and peered
contentedly from the lofty perch at their wide domain.

blue jays fussed, and they called softly to each other as their parents had before them. The winter passed for them happily.

One morning, after the spring rains had washed away the snows, and when the soft winds blew again and the flowers were awake, just at sunrise, Pansy awoke with a start. Had she heard Herman? Or was it only a dream? No, it had to be Herman. She knew it was. She followed the sound. And there he was! Herman—she knew it was—his mate, and three little hootlets were lined on the ridgepole of the old red barn! They sat blinking and warming in the early morning sun.

Pansy ran with wide-stretched arms. "Herman's come!" she cried. "Herman's come home!"

They did not hurry, but as she came closer, the owl family slowly took wing. They flew to the old marsh and settled in the tallest tree. There they sat like so many bumps, and closed their eyes to sleep.

Pansy watched them all day long. "He brought his family for me to see," she said.

HOOTLET HOME

Indeed, she could scarcely tear herself away. She watched until night settled blackly over the eaves. When morning came she ran to the marsh, but the tree had lost its peculiar bumps. The owl family had arisen early and were gone.